D1309517

DANGER ZONE:
Dieting and Eating Disorders™
BULIMIA

Stephanie Watson

ROSEN
PUBLISHING®

Published in 2007 by The Rosen Publishing Group, Inc.
29 East 21st Street, New York, NY 10010

First Edition

Library of Congress Cataloging-in-Publication Data

Watson, Stephanie, 1969–
Bulimia / Stephanie Watson.—1st ed.
     p. cm.—(Danger zone: dieting and eating disorders)
Includes bibliographical references and index.
ISBN-13: 978-1-4042-1997-7 (alk. paper)
ISBN-10: 1-4042-1997-8 (alk. paper)
1. Bulimia—Juvenile literature. I. Title.
RC552.B84W38 2007
616.85'263—dc22

                    2006033582

Manufactured in the United States of America

Contents

1

What Is Bulimia Nervosa?

Eating disorders are more than just problems with food. Having negative feelings about food can seriously affect not only how you eat but also how you interact with your friends, family, and everyone else around you. Your unhealthy relationship with food can harm both your body and your emotions.

Eating disorders include anorexia nervosa, bulimia nervosa, and binge eating disorder (also known as compulsive eating). Compulsive exercise is also a growing problem. Each disorder is slightly different, but they all pose very dangerous health risks.

Bulimia nervosa is one type of eating disorder. The word "bulimia" comes from the Greek words *buos* ("ox") and *limos* ("hunger"), which together mean "hunger of an ox."

Bulimia nervosa forces sufferers into a dangerous cycle of bingeing and purging.

People who have bulimia eat a lot of food at once (called bingeing) and then try to get rid of that food (called purging) so that they don't gain weight.

Eating disorders are more common than you might think. According to the National Eating Disorders Association, about 5 to10 million girls and women, and 1 million boys in the United States are battling an eating disorder such as

Celebrity Paula Abdul has struggled with bulimia. Media coverage of stars' battles with the illness have helped bring bulimia into the public eye.

anorexia nervosa and bulimia nervosa. And up to 15 percent of young women have unhealthy attitudes about food, reported www.girlpower.gov, a Web site sponsored by the U.S. Department of Health and Human Services. Although eating disorders are far more likely to affect young girls and women, about one out of every ten people with an eating disorder is male, according to 2006 statistics from Anorexia Nervosa and Related Eating Disorders, Inc. (ANRED).

The reasons why a person develops an eating disorder are complex. They involve eating habits, attitudes about weight and food, attitudes about body shape, and psychological factors, especially the need for control.

ABOUT BULIMIA NERVOSA

Although it was first diagnosed in the 1950s, and was probably around even before then, bulimia nervosa wasn't really understood until the 1980s. Since then, we have learned of famous people who suffered from it, including Paula Abdul, American singer and choreographer and a judge on the television show *American Idol*; and Geri Halliwell, a British singer and songwriter best known as Ginger Spice of the Spice Girls. Both of these women got help for their problem and are much healthier today.

Today, bulimia is a major social concern. It can have devastating effects on the mind and body. Many eating disorder experts believe that images in the media put a lot of pressure on young men and women to reach an "ideal" body shape—one that is impossible for most people to achieve.

Now parents, doctors, and school counselors are learning about the early warning signs of bulimia and other eating disorders in young people. Researchers are working to help people recover, but they also understand that more needs to be done to help prevent these harmful disorders in the first place.

WHAT IS BULIMIA?

Bulimia nervosa is a type of eating disorder in which a person binges and purges. Bingeing means eating a large amount of food in a short period of time. Purging means getting rid of all the food by self-induced vomiting; abuse of laxatives, diet pills, and/or diuretics; excessive exercise; or fasting.

Bingeing can mean eating a lot of calories—as many as 5,000 or more at a time. People with bulimia can binge once in a while, or twenty times each day or more. Then they will purge to rid their bodies of the extra calories. They may purge even after eating small amounts of food.

There are two types of bulimia: purging and non-purging. People with the purging type get rid of food in different ways. Some people purge by self-inducing vomiting. Others use drugs, such as diuretics (pills that increase urination), diet pills, laxatives (usually mild drugs that induce bowel movements), or enemas (liquids injected into the anus for cleansing the bowels) to clear the digestive tract. Both bingeing and purging can be experienced as intense, overwhelming urges that become uncontrollable. People with the non-purging type of bulimia exercise compulsively to get rid of the extra food they've eaten or rely on fasting.

WHO GETS BULIMIA?

It is difficult to say exactly how many people suffer from bulimia because doctors are not required to report it to health agencies. In addition, many who suffer from bulimia do not seek help. Some studies say that bulimia currently affects 1 to 3 percent of middle and high school girls and 1 to 4 percent of college women. About 10 percent of people with bulimia are male, according to the organization Anorexia Nervosa and Related Eating Disorders, Inc. Boys who are involved in activities that have them gain and lose weight quickly, such as wrestling and gymnastics, are most

Bulimia sufferers' obsession with weight can be overwhelming and all-consuming.

at risk. While most people who suffer from bulimia are in their late teens and early twenties, the disorder is affecting people at younger ages than ever before. Therapists are also seeing an increase in the numbers of middle-aged women who suffer from bulimia.

SYMPTOMS OF BULIMIA

It can be difficult to tell if a person has an eating disorder. Bulimia is especially tough to diagnose because the problem is often hidden.

Many people struggle with their relationship to food. We are taught from an early age to feel anxious and guilty around food, worry about our weight, and fear fat. People who are in the early stages of bulimia (or another eating disorder) may be overly concerned with their weight, but that isn't out of the ordinary in our culture.

People with bulimia are also not always really skinny, as you might think they would be. They can be of normal weight, or even overweight.

WARNING SIGNS OF BULIMIA

Even though people with bulimia may not look different from anyone else, there are warning signs of the condition.

What Is Bulimia Nervosa?

A person with the disorder may use extreme methods to lose weight, and may act different from how he or she used to act. It's important to recognize these warning signs so that you can help yourself or help someone else who is struggling with bulimia. An eating disorder left untreated can be life threatening. People with bulimia may do one or more of these things:

- Believe that they would be happier and more successful if they were thinner
- Have severe mood swings
- Overeat in response to stress or other uncomfortable feelings
- Alternate between strict dieting and overeating
- Go to the bathroom a lot to throw up after eating
- Exercise all the time
- Buy or steal large amounts of food
- Buy certain products, such as laxatives or syrup of ipecac (used to induce vomiting)
- Have cuts or marks on their knuckles and fingertips from using their fingers to induce vomiting
- Show other types of impulsive behavior, such as abusing drugs, going on shopping sprees, and/or shoplifting.

Myths and Facts About Bulimia

Myth: People who have bulimia only purge by forced vomiting.

Fact: People with bulimia can purge by one of several methods, including self-induced vomiting, taking laxatives, and exercising to excess.

Myth: Only people who binge eat thousands of calories in one sitting and then purge them are considered bulimic.

Fact: Eating even a small amount of food and then purging it through forced vomiting, overexercise, or laxative use can make you bulimic.

Myth: If I purge after I eat, I'll get that thin body I want.

Fact: Purging isn't likely to help you lose weight. Many people with bulimia are actually at normal weight or overweight. Purging will also cause serious damage to your body.

Myth: You can't die from bulimia.

Fact: If you deprive your body of important vitamins and minerals, you can become very sick. Low potassium or an electrolyte imbalance in your body can cause your heart to stop beating, which will cause you to die. Medical experts, including those at the National Institutes of Health, estimate that the death rate for people with eating disorders is about 20 percent.

Myth: If you have bulimia, you'll never recover.

Fact: With treatment, most people can recover from bulimia. The sooner you get help, the better your chances of recovery. Some people who have undergone treatment for bulimia have been able to recover fully.

HOW IS BULIMIA DIFFERENT FROM ANOREXIA?

Although they are different disorders, anorexia and bulimia share many of the same symptoms. This is the reason why "nervosa" is part of both terms. In fact, about 50 percent of people who have bulimia had anorexia first. In both cases, the person is preoccupied with dieting, food, weight, and body size.

But there are also a few differences. People with anorexia refuse to eat. They also deny to themselves and to others that there is a problem. People with bulimia usually eat, but then purge. They are aware that there is a problem, even though they may try to keep it a secret from others.

People with anorexia are 15 percent below the recommended weight for their size. Those with bulimia are usually of average weight, though they may weigh ten or fifteen pounds (4.5 or 6.8 kilograms) above or below the average.

Keeping bingeing and purging a secret can add to a bulimic's sense of loneliness and despair.

EMOTIONS AND BULIMIA

When people purge, they are not just getting rid of food. They are also trying to get rid of unwanted feelings like anxiety, anger, guilt, panic, and stress. And it doesn't take very long for the bingeing and purging habit to become an addictive pattern.

Although scientists are still researching this idea, some believe purging may affect chemicals in the brain, causing a person to feel satisfied after an episode. A person with bulimia repeats the cycle to feel the same rush after purging. They believe that purging is the only way to get those feelings again.

Bulimia turns the act of eating into a self-destructive behavior. Eating stops being a pleasurable experience. Food is instead used to deal with uncomfortable feelings like fear, anger, and guilt. People with bulimia are unable to stop the secret cycle of bingeing and purging because they rely upon this ritual to handle their feelings. Soon it has taken over their lives.

No matter how thin they are, people with bulimia always fear that they will get fat. They feel that being thin means being happy.

People with bulimia are unable to deal with uncomfortable feelings. They see their bodies as being much larger than they really are. As a result, they refuse to eat in a healthy way and use dangerous methods to lose weight.

WHO IS AT RISK?

Anyone can develop an eating disorder. While it affects mostly white, middle- to upper-class females, it can happen to males and females of all races, classes, and ages. It can happen to good students who are popular, and successful adults who hold good jobs. But it also can happen to people who have problems, such as drug or alcohol addiction, as well as people who have been sexually abused or suffer from depression.

Athletes are also at risk for eating disorders, especially those who are in sports that connect weight with performance. It can be a problem for dancers, weight lifters, wrestlers, gymnasts, swimmers, and long-distance runners. Teens in competitive soccer leagues are also at risk. Young men with eating disorders may be reluctant to get help. They may feel that an eating disorder is a "female problem" and be too embarrassed to tell anyone about it.

2

Why Do People Develop Bulimia?

Everyone overeats at some point or another. We have all eaten too much on certain occasions or during the holidays, and that's normal. The difference is that someone with bulimia will do it on a regular basis and cannot control the urge to binge.

An eating disorder like bulimia is very complicated. There is no one cause—there are many different factors that contribute to it. Just because you feel out of control about life does not mean that you will develop an eating disorder, though. Often there are many other things happening in a person's life that trigger the problem.

The person who is experiencing it usually does not consciously decide to develop an eating disorder. It's an unconscious process. The bottom line is that the eating disorder itself is actually an expression of other problems in a person's life. It may be a way for them to feel some sense of control. It may be a way for them to feel a sense of identity, independence, or even security. It may be a way for them to compulsively repeat abusive situations, that is, to take in painful amounts of food while being able to then say "no" and to purge.

OUTSIDE INFLUENCES

Bulimia, as well as other eating disorders, tends to be triggered by family and relationship problems. It can start as a result of a comment about your weight from a parent or a friend, or if you're an athlete, from a coach. Bulimia can also be a symptom of a larger problem, such as depression, low self-esteem, sexual abuse, and family dysfunction.

Bulimia usually develops at a time in a person's life when a big change is taking place. This could be your parents' divorce, moving to another town, changing schools, or going off to college. It could also be a trauma, such as rape or sexual assault. Dramatic experiences that happen during the teen years, when young people are already experiencing major changes in their bodies, could trigger an eating disorder.

18

MEDIA

One of the main issues that eating disorder experts agree on is the negative influence magazines, advertising, and television have on people's body image. Constantly seeing images of perfect models can have harmful effects on a person's self-esteem.

The problem is that movies, television, and all forms of advertising make people feel that there is an ideal way their bodies should look in order to be worthy and acceptable to others. Everywhere you look, from billboards to TV ads,

Media images can add to the pressure to be thin. Developing realistic weight goals can set you up for success instead of frustration.

there is pressure to diet and be thin. Americans spend billions of dollars each year on dieting, from weight-loss centers to diet pills and diet books. Advertisers constantly try to convince us, with ads for everything from diet sodas to bathing suits, that if you eat, you'll get fat.

And for many people, there is nothing worse than being fat. One survey by Eating Disorders Awareness and Prevention, Inc. (EDAP, now called the National Eating Disorders Association [NEDA]) reported that young girls are more afraid of becoming fat than they are of cancer, nuclear war, or losing their parents.

The media sends strong messages to young women that they are fat no matter what size they happen to be. As a result, many females, and an increasing number of males, have a distorted body image. They think they need to lose weight, when in fact, they are very healthy at their current body size.

FAMILY ISSUES

Research has shown that young children will eat only when they're hungry. They naturally control how much they eat. But parents soon interfere with their children's eating patterns. When this happens, children learn to eat for reasons other than hunger.

Parental influence makes food take on a different meaning. For example, you learn at a very young age what is okay to eat after school or what is not allowed before dinner. You may be told that candy and other sweets are "bad" for you, but you are given such foods as rewards for "good" behavior, such as playing fair or doing well in school.

Parents also influence their children's eating in other ways. Sometimes, parents who are concerned about their own weight cause their children to worry about their weight, too. Or, a mother may keep telling her daughter that she has to be thinner to look good. One study found that 40 percent of nine- to ten-year-old girls lose weight when their mothers ask them to do so. A 2005 study found that teenaged girls whose mothers valued thinness were more likely to themselves want to be thin and to diet. Fathers also can have a big effect on the way their daughters eat if they're very critical, studies show.

Bulimia may also run in families. Researchers think that bulimia and other eating disorders are linked to genes. This means if one of your family members suffers from an eating disorder, you may be at a higher risk for developing one as well. In 2002, a group of researchers at Virginia Commonwealth University and the University of Pittsburgh Medical Center found an area on one particular chromosome (the structure that contains the genes) that was common to families with a history of bulimia. Medical researchers are continuing to investigate bulimia's genetic link.

DRUG AND ALCOHOL ABUSE

Research shows that people with eating disorders are more likely to have parents who abuse alcohol or drugs. In a home in which a parent is an alcoholic or drug abuser, children live in an almost constant state of disorder. They may never know from one minute to the next how their parent will act. They may be afraid to have friends visit. They may spend lots of time alone taking care of themselves.

An eating disorder may be a cry for help in this lonely situation. Or, it may be a way to take control of some part of your life—over what you eat, how much you eat, and even how you rid your body of food.

PHYSICAL ABUSE

Sexual and physical abuse have also been linked to eating disorders. Research studies reported in 2002 have indicted that as many as 35 percent of women with bulimia were sexually abused. The abusers might be a parent, a friend, a relative, or another trusted adult.

The betrayal and pain that comes from being abused can lead to severe emotional problems. The eating disorder can be a way to bury those painful feelings and ease the emotional pain. People who are sexually abused grow up with little or no sense of control over their own bodies. Bulimia is an attempt to regain control.

Bulimia in the case of abuse may also be a way for people to punish themselves because they feel they don't deserve to be happy. When people don't feel worthy enough to express what they want, they can start bingeing and purging behaviors. Bingeing is a way to express their desires, and purging is like punishing themselves for trying to fulfill those desires.

PERSONAL INFLUENCES

How you feel about yourself and your body can affect your eating habits. People who have bulimia may have certain personality traits that lead to destructive eating behaviors.

One trait is perfectionism: wanting to do everything just right and being very hard on yourself if you make a mistake. Another trait is self-loathing: you see a fat, ugly person every time you look in the mirror, even if everyone else sees you as thin and pretty. Many people with bulimia are also depressed. They feel sad a lot, and they withdraw from family and friends.

DIETING

What happens when people feel that they're not good enough because they're not thin enough? They usually think a diet is the answer to all their problems. But diets are dangerous because they set up an unhealthy relationship with food. In fact, while not all diets lead to eating disorders, adolescents who are serious dieters are eighteen times more likely to develop an eating disorder than those who don't diet, according to the National Association of Anorexia Nervosa and Associated Disorders.

Bulimics may have an unrealistic or inaccurate view of how they look. They may hate what they see in the mirror even if others perceive them as attractive.

Diets are not always healthy. When people restrict their food intake, they are depriving themselves. This can cause them to become obsessed with everything they feel they are missing. It is natural for the body to rebel against a diet.

When your body is deprived of food, it reacts as if it were being attacked. Your metabolism slows down, and your body burns fewer calories. This is because your body is trying to hold on to the little food it's getting. The body reacts to dieting by storing fat more efficiently to survive.

When people with bulimia break their diets, they often binge. Breaking a diet can cause feelings of guilt. The only way to relieve that guilt is to purge.

DEPRESSION

When people are depressed, they feel very sad. It is common to feel depressed sometimes. But some people can feel depressed for weeks at a time or they can feel a little depressed for years. There are many forms of depression, and usually there is no one reason for it. Often many factors are involved in a person's depression. It could be a medical condition or the drugs that are being prescribed for its treatment that causes the depression. Or perhaps there's a stressful problem within the social environment, such as an unpleasant family situation or homelessness, that contributes to the depression. Perhaps there is a family history of depression—although people who have genetic links to the condition may not get depressed. Or maybe a certain life event, such as a death in the family, causes the depression. Even certain patterns of thinking can affect the way a person reacts to some situations. Depression has many symptoms. People who are depressed may be very tired, have trouble concentrating or sleeping, feel hopeless, and even think about killing themselves. Depression can also affect appetite, and people who suffer from depression often develop bulimia. Experts are studying the link between eating disorders and depression. Many doctors have found that some types of antidepressant medications, such as fluoxetine (Prozac), have been effective in reducing the occurrences of bingeing and purging while treating bulimic patients. The Mayo Clinic indicated in a March 2006 report that combining antidepressant medications with cognitive behavior therapy (a kind of psychotherapy that is used to treat depression, anxiety, and other forms of mental disorder) seemed to be the most helpful method of treating bulimia.

3

How Bulimia Affects the Body and Mind

Bulimia, like all eating disorders, can have very harmful effects on the mind and body. It's important to understand the dangers of this disorder so you can get treatment for yourself, a family member, or a friend.

BULIMIA AND THE BODY

Bulimia can be very hard on the body. It can harm almost every organ, from the heart to the skin. If bulimia is left untreated, a person may need to be hospitalized. The longer the eating disorder remains untreated, the worse the problems become.

HEALTH PROBLEMS FROM BULIMIA

About half of the women with bulimia have an irregular menstrual cycle (also called a period) or stop having their period altogether, according to the American Academy of Family Physicians. Not getting a period is called amenorrhea. Studies have found that not menstruating can cause other problems as well. Women who don't get their periods lack enough estrogen, which helps maintain strong bones. A lack of estrogen can cause osteoporosis, a disease that weakens the bones. When the bones are weak, they break easily. Other health problems that can be caused by bulimia include:

- Irregular heartbeat
- Low blood pressure
- Dehydration
- Vitamin and mineral imbalances
- Irregular bowel movements
- Diarrhea
- Abdominal cramps
- Dizziness
- Swelling of the cheeks
- Gum disease
- Cavities (erosion of tooth enamel)
- Sore throat and esophagus due to stomach acid
- Cuts on knuckles (from biting the skin with the teeth during forced vomiting)

THE FEMALE ATHLETE TRIAD

For some athletes, bulimia can cause a condition that doctors call the female athlete triad. The word "triad" refers to the three health problems that occur together in many female athletes: disordered eating, loss of menstrual periods, and loss of bone mass. Any one of these conditions can signal that the body's essential nutrients and tissues are being raided, usually by a combination of starvation and overexercising.

When all three conditions appear at the same time, it is a health emergency. Experts aren't sure exactly how many women have the female athlete triad. But a British study found that as many as 15 to 60 percent of female athletes in sports such as gymnastics, long-distance running, and figure skating have disordered eating, and as many as 50 percent of these women overexercise.

VITAMIN AND MINERAL LOSS

When you vomit after eating, you lose the vitamins, minerals, and other nutrients that would normally be absorbed into your body. Not eating normally can throw your body into emergency mode. After a few days, you will start using up your fat deposits and then muscle. To keep going, your body will rob nutrients from organs such as the liver and

Bulimia can cause dizziness, fatigue, and stomach pains, which can be accompanied by bloating and cramping.

heart. You also lose water when you vomit, which can lead to dehydration.

Dehydration from purging causes dry skin, brittle nails and hair, and hair loss. A lack of vitamins and minerals such as iron, phosphorous, and potassium in the body can put a person at risk for malnutrition even if that person is not too thin and eats regular meals at other times. Not having enough of these vitamins and minerals can make a person feel tired. It can also cause skin problems, weak eyesight, and damage to the heart, kidneys, and bones.

The most serious side effect of bulimia is an electrolyte imbalance. Repeated purging causes a depletion of the electrolytes potassium, chlorine, and sodium. These are electrically charged ions necessary for all of the body's major systems to function. An electrolyte imbalance can cause kidney problems, muscle spasms, heart irregularities, and even death.

STOMACH AND ORGAN TROUBLE

Vomiting is a violent reflex that batters the esophagus and stomach lining. The damage is invisible, but it is so serious that it can become painful to swallow anything, even water. Over time, it gets hard to keep any food down. The body will purge as an automatic reflex after eating. In severe cases, the lining of the esophagus will wear away. A hole in the esophagus can cause sudden death.

All of this stomach damage from purging can cause pain, cramps, and indigestion. Using laxatives can also cause painful spasms in the intestines, and using them too often can actually make a person constipated to the point that they depend on laxatives to have normal bowel movements.

OUTWARD SIGNS OF BULIMIA

Not only does bulimia cause problems inside the body, it also leaves more obvious symptoms on the outside. The pressure of repeated vomiting can cause blood vessels in the face (especially in and around the eyes), legs, and arms to break, leaving little red lines in the skin. Purging can also cause puffiness and swelling in the hands, feet, or face. And purging can cause the salivary glands in the face to enlarge, making the cheeks look swollen.

Vomiting over and over brings stomach acids up into the mouth. These acids are strong enough to break down foods. They are also strong enough to wear away tooth enamel and the softer tissues of the mouth. They can leave holes or raggedy edges in the teeth and can make the gums swollen and tender. People who vomit a lot are likely to develop tooth decay and gum disease, and could lose many teeth.

Using laxatives can cause repeated diarrhea. This can lead to a condition called rectal prolapse, in which part of your colon comes out through your rectum. It may need to be fixed surgically.

BULIMIA AND THE MIND

When all of your time and energy is focused on weight and what you are or aren't eating, it can take a big emotional toll on your life. It can affect your relationships with your family and friends, and make you miss out on the things you once loved to do.

EMOTIONAL TOLL

People suffering from bulimia often feel guilty and ashamed. Bingeing and purging can cause intense and over-whelming feelings of anxiety and tension. There is also fear when people realize they are hurting their bodies. Most frightening of all is the belief that there is no way to make it all stop.

Bulimia can have a big effect on personality. Many people who have bulimia have mood swings. They may be happy and upbeat when they feel in control, then hopeless and depressed when they feel like they've eaten too much or lost control. The depression that often comes with bulimia can

Bulimia puts both your physical and mental health in jeopardy. It diverts your energy and attention from friends, schoolwork, and the activities you used to enjoy.

drain them of their energy and make them stay home alone rather than going out with friends.

RITUALS AND SELF-IMAGE

How much you eat and what you do after you eat it (like purging) can become rituals. People with bulimia become very protective of their rituals. They may not want to get help because it means giving up the behaviors that make them feel like they're in control. Really, though, they are becoming more and more out of control as the disease progresses. Some of the rituals people with bulimia may perform are going to the bathroom often after meals, hiding large amounts of food and bingeing, and exercising constantly even in bad weather.

People with bulimia have a distorted self-image because they often have little contact with other people. They may also be very depressed about what they are doing to themselves. These feelings can be devastating. In the worst cases, a person may consider suicide as the only way out. That's why it's so important that a person with bulimia talks to someone—a friend, family member, teacher, or counselor—and get help right away.

4

Recovering from Bulimia

Many people who suffer from bulimia are so caught up in the cycle that they don't know how or whom to ask for help. To recover from an eating disorder, you have to learn what caused it and how to deal with your problems in a healthier way. And the earlier you deal with those problems, the easier it is to get better.

GETTING HELP

If you think you may suffer from an eating disorder, it's extremely important to get professional help. It's also important to remember that you are not alone and help is available.

Consider speaking with someone you trust, such as a parent, friend, or counselor. You can also contact one of the eating disorder organizations for more information and help.

Treating bulimia can be a long and complicated process. Some people who formerly suffered from bulimia have said that recovering from bulimia was the toughest job they've ever had. It may take as long as six months to two years in treatment before a person can stop the binge-purge cycle, but there is no specific time frame for recovery. The longer someone has had bulimia, the harder it is to break the habits. The earlier it is treated, the better the chances are for recovery.

There are no laboratory tests specifically designed to detect bulimia, but the doctor may run tests to see what effects the eating disorder has had on a person's body. Blood tests can be done to check for potassium deficiency and other electrolyte imbalances. The doctor may also take a chest radiograph to look for signs that the esophagus has ruptured, an electrocardiogram to check how well the heart is working, and a thyroid test to make sure the thyroid gland is functioning properly.

HEALING THE BODY

There is no single way to recover from bulimia and there are no miracle cures. You may have to try a few different types of treatment before one works for you. Although some people recover without therapy, most need some type of help.

The first part of treatment for bulimia is to get your body healthy again. If the situation is a medical emergency, you may have to go to the hospital. This will happen if you are bingeing and purging several times every day, are dehydrated or have an electrolyte imbalance, or feel suicidal.

You may be given fluids and nutrients through a vein in your arm until you are strong enough to eat on your own. Your doctor may give you an antinausea drug that will reduce your urge to vomit. You may also get an antacid to decrease stomach acids. And a nutritionist may work with you to get your eating back on a healthy track.

HEALING THE MIND

The first and most effective treatment for bulimia is behavioral therapy. Therapy can be done individually, with family, or in groups. A technique called cognitive-behavioral therapy is very effective for treating bulimia. This therapy helps people understand why they developed bulimia in the first place and teaches them how to change their thinking and behavior so that they can stop it from continuing.

Danger Zone: Bulimia

Because depression is common in people with bulimia, sometimes doctors prescribe drugs called antidepressants. These drugs help people deal with depression and other feelings bulimia can cause. Antidepressants should only be used by people who are of normal weight or who are overweight, though, because they can cause weight loss. The most common antidepressants are the selective serotonin reuptake inhibitors (SSRIs). These include Prozac, Zoloft, and Paxil. They work by affecting chemicals in the brain that are involved in mood.

Bulimia can have an impact on a whole family since it affects how the sufferer does, or does not, interact with other family members. To be effective, the recovery process might need to involve the whole family, too.

FAMILY THERAPY

The families of people with bulimia may need help healing, too. Family therapy can help improve relationships while the person with the eating disorder recovers.

For families in which a problem such as abuse contributed to the eating disorder, treatment is even more important. Someone who is in recovery cannot get better if they continue to live with an abusive family. When a family problem, such as divorce or death, cannot be changed, the recovering person must learn new ways to cope.

GROUP THERAPY

Talking to people who have had similar experiences can help you work through your feelings and come to terms with your disorder. This is called group therapy, or a support group. Group therapy can be a powerful process. Knowing you're not the only one with bulimia can help you feel less ashamed. It is also very comforting to be able to talk about your pain with people who will understand because they, too, have lived through it.

Support groups are an important part of eating disorder treatment. There are many different types of support groups and they are all very effective if the participants are willing to work hard to get well.

HELPING A LOVED ONE WHO HAS BULIMIA

You may notice some of the warning signs of an eating disorder (binge eating, self-induced vomiting, perfectionist behavior) in a friend or relative. If you do, speak up. It may not be easy to do. It can feel as if you are betraying a loved one. But the person needs help. Approach your friend gently, tell him or her that you're worried, and listen sympathetically.

Try to understand that your friend may not admit she or he has a problem. If that happens, don't force your friend to get help. Give your friend support. You can give the person a list of places to go for help or people to call, including the school guidance counselor. Even if your friend doesn't want help, he or she may keep the list and use it later.

If your friend is not listening to you, and you feel it is an emergency situation, confide in a trusted adult—a teacher, nurse, guidance counselor, friend, or family member. An

It might take time for a friend or family member to admit he or she has a problem. You can help by providing support and resources to get your loved one on the path to recovery.

emergency situation is if your friend is vomiting blood, has a very severe stomachache, vomits several times each day, or talks about suicide. Your friend may be angry, but you should react immediately because your friend's life is in danger.

STAYING HEALTHY

Remember that bulimia is a chronic illness. Even with treatment, the condition can return. It is not easy to recover, but it is possible with help. If you are willing to help yourself, you'll have a better chance of recovering.

Up to 20 percent of people who don't get treatment for eating disorders die, according to Anorexia Nervosa and Related Eating Disorders, Inc. (ANRED). With treatment, about 97 to 98 percent survive.

RECOVERY

ANRED has also indicated that about 60 percent of people with eating disorders can recover if they get treatment. This is why receiving treatment is so important if you are suffering from bulimia.

With treatment, you can learn how to eat well to keep your body at a healthy weight. You can get back into your regular routine with school, activities, and friends. Most of all, you can start to feel better about yourself.

THE CHANCE OF RELAPSE

Even with treatment, not everyone with bulimia will recover for good. Often people have many setbacks. As reported in 2006 by ANRED, just under half of the people with bulimia don't improve, or continue to have some problems throughout their lives. Some people recovering from bulimia will have to worry about relapse in the same way that a person with an addiction to alcohol must deal with relapse. It is a very real part of the recovery process.

When people have a drug or alcohol addiction, the most important part of their treatment is to stop using those chemicals. They can avoid situations where they might be tempted to use them. But people with bulimia cannot stay away from food. They need to eat. A treatment program can help them learn to eat in a healthy way.

5

Developing a Positive Body Image

There are many things you can do to prevent eating disorders. Many experts believe the sooner you work to change your self-image, the better you will be at handling many of life's challenges and avoiding the possible dangers of eating disorders.

If you find yourself starting to spend a lot of time thinking or talking about food, your weight, calories, and dieting, talk to a parent or someone else you trust. It's also time to talk to someone if you exercise constantly or always avoid activities that make you feel self-conscious about your weight.

PREVENTING EATING DISORDERS

The first step to preventing an eating disorder is to accept and love your body. It's not an easy thing to do

A positive self-image can be a big step toward preventing an eating disorder.

because we live in a culture that rewards the thin and punishes the fat. But that doesn't mean that you have to listen to or believe these harmful messages. You are not powerless against them.

With a little help from family, friends, doctors, and counselors, you can begin to love who you are right now, instead of who you wish you could be. There are many

Friends can help each other celebrate who they are and how they look.

ways that you can fight back and help prevent eating disorders—both in yourself and in others.

TAKE CHARGE OF YOUR EMOTIONS

If you are experiencing uncomfortable feelings or if something has changed in your life—your parents recently divorced, a family member is ill, or a good friend moved away—don't hide your feelings. Find someone to talk to about what's on your mind. A school guidance counselor is a good place to start. Some towns have local hotlines for teens to call if they need someone to talk to. Some schools have peer support groups, so you can talk to your class-mates about your concerns. Try to talk to your parents or anyone else you trust. Never keep your worries a secret.

TAKE CARE OF YOUR BODY

In addition to improving your mental outlook, you also need to take care of your body. It's not easy always to eat healthy foods. But making a real lifestyle change takes a bit of work.

A healthy exercise and nutrition plan is good for your mind and body.

Ten Great Questions to Ask When You're Asking for Help

Before you go to a doctor or counselor, write down these questions and bring them with you. They are a good guide to help you start a conversation with the people who will help you recover.

1. Do I have bulimia?

2. What effects has bingeing and purging had on my body?

3. What tests will I have to take to check my health?

4. What treatments do I have to choose from?

5. How can I deal with my negative self-image?

6. Can I take medication, and what effects will it have on me?

7. How can I control my urges to binge and purge?

8. What is the best way for me to eat a healthy diet?

9. As I recover from bulimia, what exercises should I be doing to stay in shape and how often should I be doing them so I don't go overboard?

10. How do I deal with the emotional issues in my life that led to my bulimia?

Fad diets, pills, and bingeing and purging offer quick fixes, but there are much healthier ways to lose weight and get in shape. The problem with fad diets and diet pills is they don't teach you to change your eating habits so that you eat right most of the time. If you eat a well-balanced diet that includes proteins, dairy, fruits, vegetables, and grains,

Exercise can be a healthy way to help maintain your weight, but make sure you don't overdo it! You don't want to replace one obsession with another.

your body will be healthy. And that's much more important than what the numbers say on your scale.

Remember your body shape and size is determined mostly by genetics. You have only so much control over what your body looks like. Look at yourself as an individual with very unique characteristics. Try not to compare yourself to an unrealistic ideal. Also remember that you are focusing on learning new and healthy eating habits. If you make healthy eating a natural part of your life, you can protect yourself against the dangerous habits that lead to an eating disorder, and you can learn to love your body and the person inside it!

And don't forget to exercise, too. If you don't want to join a gym, take a bike ride or walk or jog in your neighborhood three times every week, or buy exercise videos and work out right at home. The important thing is to focus on all the wonderful things your body can do, not what you think is wrong with it.

If you're concerned about your weight, talk to your parents or your doctor. The doctor can help you plan out a diet and exercise program that's right for you.

FIGHT BACK AGAINST EATING DISORDERS

Remember that preventing eating disorders is a fight, and you are not powerless in that fight. You have the right to stand up and rebel against society's endless quest to be thin. You have the right to react to those waiflike models on television and refuse to be like them.

WRITE A LETTER

You are a consumer and should feel free to speak out against weight discrimination in the media. Don't like what

you see in the latest issue of your favorite magazine? Tell them what you think. If you don't see the changes you want, stop buying it. You can send a message to advertisers when you make decisions about what you will and won't buy. If you see something on television that upsets you, write a letter to the network. Network executives do care about what viewers think.

People often find that fighting against society's messages helps them change their own beliefs. Fighting back can provide a release for all those negative thoughts you may be experiencing.

REBEL AGAINST DIET CULTURE

People out there are starting to challenge society's thinking about weight. Today, there are e-zines (magazines that are published on the Internet), newsletters, magazines, and books promoting the idea that all body shapes are beautiful.

There are many organizations you can join to help fight against diet culture. The National Eating Disorders

Learning to eat in a healthy way again after a battle with bulimia can take time.

Association (NEDA) organizes Eating Disorders Awareness Week, the first week of February every year. They call the Friday of that week "Fearless Friday." On that day, everyone agrees not to diet, but instead to eat in a healthy way.

STOP NEGATIVE TALK

It's easy to fall into the trap of talking negatively about yourself. But stop and think about what you are saying. Would you say those things to a friend or a family member? It's important to talk to yourself the way you would to a loved one.

You and your friends can help build each other's self-esteem. Seeing the best in others is good practice for seeing the best in yourself.

Changing these inner thoughts takes time, but it's important to value yourself for the qualities that matter, such as generosity, sensitivity, and intelligence—things that make you a unique individual. The next time you start to put yourself down, say something positive instead. For example, "I look good in this dress," or "I value the person I am inside."

Remember, the changes you make now will help you keep a positive self-image in the future. Invest in yourself. You are worth it!

Glossary

addiction An obsessive-compulsive need for and use of a substance or behavior.

amenorrhea When a woman who is not pregnant stops getting her period.

antidepressant A drug to relieve or prevent depression.

binge To eat uncontrollably.

calorie A unit for measuring the energy that food supplies to the body.

dehydration The loss of an excessive amount of water or body fluids.

depression A feeling of sadness that lasts a long time and may need to be treated with the help of therapy and/or medication.

diuretic A drug that causes an increase in the amount of urine the kidneys produce.

electrolyte imbalance A serious condition in which a person doesn't have enough of the minerals necessary for healthy body function.

esophagus The tube through which food passes from your throat to your stomach.

estrogen A female hormone.

Glossary

fasting Going for a period of time without eating any food.

genetic Relating to how people inherit traits and appearances from their parents.

laxative A substance that brings on a bowel movement.

menstrual cycle A female's monthly cycle, including the making of hormones, the thickening of the uterine lining, and the shedding of the uterine lining, that ends with menstrual bleeding (menstruation). It's the cycle during which an egg develops and is released from an ovary and the uterus is prepared to receive a fertilized egg.

nutrients Proteins, minerals, and vitamins that a person needs to live and grow.

osteoporosis A condition in which the bones become fragile.

psychological Having to do with the mind.

puberty The time when your body becomes sexually mature.

purge To clear the body of food, usually through forced vomiting, excessive exercise, or laxatives.

relapse A recurrence of symptoms of a disease or condition from which there has been improvement.

Resources

Anorexia Nervosa and Related Eating Disorders, Inc. (ANRED)

www.anred.com

ANRED is a nonprofit group that can teach you more about bulimia and other eating disorders, and help you recover from your disorder.

Eating Disorder Referral and Information Center

www.edreferral.com

This searchable database can help you find an eating disorder specialist in your area.

gURL

www.gurl.com

An online magazine for young women that talks honestly about body image.

National Eating Disorders Association (NEDA)

603 Stewart Street, Suite 803

Seattle, WA 98101

(800) 931-2237

www.edap.org

NEDA is the largest nonprofit organization that works to prevent and to help people suffering from bulimia and other eating disorders.

Resources

National Institute of Mental Health (NIMH)

6001 Executive Boulevard, Room 8184, MSC 9663

Bethesda, MD 20892-9663

(866) 615-6464

www.nimh.nih.gov

The NIMH helps people learn about all aspects of mental health, including eating disorders.

The National Women's Health Information Center

U.S. Department of Health and Human Services

(800) 994-9662

www.4woman.gov/faq/Easyread/bulnervosa-etr.htm

An easy-to-read information sheet on bulimia, its causes, and its effects on the body.

WEB SITES

Due to the changing nature of Internet links, Rosen Publishing has developed an online list of Web sites related to the subject of this book. This site is updated regularly. Please use this link to access the list:

http://www.rosenlinks.com/dz/buli

For Further Reading

Bell, Julia. *Massive*. New York, NY: Simon & Schuster, 2006.

Eliot, Eve. *Insatiable: The Compelling Story of Four Teens, Food, and Its Power*. Deerfield Beach, FL: Health Communications, Inc., 2004.

Friend, Natasha. *Perfect*. Minneapolis, MN: Milkweed Editions, 2004.

Golden, Jocelyn. *Learning to Be Me: My Twenty-Three-Year Battle with Bulimia*. Lincoln, NE: iUniverse, Inc., 2005.

Hall, Lindsey, and Leigh Cohn. *Bulimia: A Guide to Recovery*. 5th ed. Carlsbad, CA: Gurze Books, 1999.

Hornbacher, Marya. *Wasted: A Memoir of Anorexia and Bulimia*. New York, NY: Harper Perennial, 2006.

Kramer, Gerri Freid. *The Truth About Eating Disorders*. Mark J. Kittleson, general ed. New York, NY: Facts on File, 2004.

Lawton, Sandra A. *Eating Disorders Information for Teens: Health Tips About Anorexia, Bulimia, Binge Eating, and Other Eating Disorders* (Teen Health Series). Detroit, MI: Omnigraphics, 2005.

McCabe, Randi E., Traci L. McFarlane, and Marion P. Olmstead. *Overcoming Bulimia: Your Comprehensive,*

Step-by-Step Guide to Recovery. Oakland, CA: New Harbinger Publications, 2004.

McClure, Cynthia Rowland. *The Monster Within: Facing an Eating Disorder*. Grand Rapids, MI: Revell, 2002.

Reindl, Sheila M. *Sensing the Self: Women's Recovery from Bulimia*. Cambridge, MA: Harvard University Press, 2002.

Index

A

amenorrhea, 28
anorexia nervosa, 4, 13–14
Anorexia Nervosa and Related
    Eating Disorders, Inc., 6, 9, 42, 43
athletes, and eating disorders, 9, 16,
    18, 29

B

behavioral therapy, 37
binge eating disorder, 4
body, taking care of your, 47–51
body image, 20, 44–45, 51
bulimia nervosa
    described, 5, 8
    emotions and, 15, 23, 33–34
    genetics and, 21–22
    health problems caused by, 27–34
    helping someone with, 40–42
    myths and facts about, 12–13
    origin of name, 4
    questions to ask about, 48–49
    reasons people develop, 15–16,
        17–26
    recovery from, 35–43
    relapse and, 43
    rituals and, 34
    treatment of, 26, 36–39, 42
    types of, 8

warning signs of, 10–11, 40
who gets it, 9–10, 16

C

celebrities, and eating disorders, 7

D

depression, 16, 18, 24, 25–26,
    33–34, 38
dieting, 8, 11, 20, 24–25, 44, 49
    society and, 53–54
diuretics, 8
drug and alcohol abuse, 16, 22, 43

E

eating disorders
    death from, 13, 31, 42
    effect on relationships of, 4, 32
    genetics and, 21–22
    preventing, 44–55
    statistics on, 5–6, 22, 24
    types of, 4
    why they develop, 6
electrolyte imbalance, 13, 30–31,
    36, 37
esophagus, damage to, 31, 36
exercise, 51

Index

PHOTO CREDITS